Where Healing Starts

Bhon Glory Jayn P. Cabilete

Ukiyoto Publishing

All global publishing rights are held by

Ukiyoto Publishing

Published in 2024

Content Copyright © Bhon Glory Jayn P. Cabilete
Cover Illustration by: Jozef Guantero
ISBN 9789367957820

*All rights reserved.
No part of this publication may be reproduced,
transmitted, or stored in a retrieval system, in any form
by any means, electronic, mechanical, photocopying,
recording or otherwise, without the prior permission of
the publisher.*

The moral rights of the authors have been asserted.

*This is a work of fiction. Names, characters, businesses,
places, events, locales, and incidents are either the
products of the author's imagination or used in a fictitious
manner. Any resemblance to actual persons, living or
dead, or actual events is purely coincidental.*

*This book is sold subject to the condition that it shall not by
way of trade or otherwise, be lent, resold, hired out or
otherwise circulated, without the publisher's prior
consent, in any form of binding or cover other than that in
which it is published.*

www.ukiyoto.com

"Did you eat the tarts and put the crusts there?"
— Queen Elsemere, Mirana and Iracebeth's mother, in *Alice Through the Looking Glass (2016)*, directed by James Bobin and adapted from Lewis Carroll's *Alice's Adventures in Wonderland (1865)*

The Menu

Table Cloth: A Short Introduction   1

Part One - The Surface: Served On Top   5
  The Manananggal's Noche Buena   *7*
  Café Latte   *13*
  Let's Eat Lechon in a Doll House   *17*
  Behind the Steps of Cooking Ginisang Kalabasa   *21*

Part Two - The Bottom: Served Below   25
  The Lockdown Offering   *27*
  Pizza Delivery   *31*
  Happy Birthday   *39*
  Devoured by Death   *47*

The Kitchen: A Brief Outro   55
Words After Eating: Acknowledgement   57

About the Author   59

Table Cloth: A Short Introduction

I have been astonished that the common saying, "food brings us together," is pertinent that it is used as a tagline when a gathering is taking place. From within a family in the dining room to a grand feast like fiestas, reunions or birthdays, food becomes the emulsifier, either through a dessert, a meal, or perhaps a beverage. Every aspect of it resonates with themes of joy and reflects the nuances of our social reality that it has its own nutritional matter to bind people and its unhealthy composition that breaks relationships. Food has the ability to dictate the value of human connection to one another; it becomes a significant element in how we deplete things around us, either in a real sense from the food or from the idea of consuming something.

The stories that you are about to read contain deficiencies that are raw on the reader's mind as they slowly uncover their version of a culinarian or a food lover. These fictional stories are by-products that go beyond the sole definition of food to be the feature of sustenance, as I acknowledge that there is something underneath what food could actually offer to human affinities. A specific food's savor may taste dissimilar when shared with a different person. Also, imagine yourself drinking the same coffee twice. The taste of that particular coffee may have the same aroma. Still, it is ingested differently according to its intent and the occasion, thus making the flavor likely distinct and barely detectable at some point, especially when the first one was downed while reading a personal book and the other was consumed while having a business meeting.

I even heard common conversations that goes similar to like:

"Hearing your words already makes me full."

"Knowledge is the best sustenance."

"I have a suggestion! We should…"

These lines go with the concept of "food for thought," and these give an impression that food is indeed beyond what we can only bite, chew, and swallow nor drink. Even death could also be a chef who devours the undercooked love between forbidden lovers and innocent superstitions. The presented concept of food being a nonhuman thing is a reality that brings multiple interpretations of its role in our lives, especially in the direction of humankind.

May you discover the inner *chef* hidden beneath your soul and enjoy being a *food lover* as you grapple with the stories that you are about to read, *where hunger waits* at the tip of your fingertips when you flip the pages.

— Glory Cabilete —

Part One - The Surface: Served On Top

The *Manananggal's Noche Buena*

It's finally the last week of October. A few days down the road, the town's Halloween spirit will be encapsulated in chocolates and candy. I am looking forward to seeing kids dressed as ghosts or frightening costumes as they go door-to-door or even store-to-store in a mall in search of sweets.

The sound of children's voices shouting, "Trick or Treat!" in harmony coupled with repeated door knocking woke me up one morning. *It's still too early!* I stand up, grab a box of Nips chocolates from the fridge, and rub my eyes before I walk like a drunk person. I quickly opened the door to give the sweets to the children. I stun; I can't tell whether I am staring outside my apartment or into a hollow mirror. Their smiles are as charming as the childhood memories I wish to be wrapped in plastic.

Suddenly, they vanish into thin air as soon as I stop staring at them. I just rub my eyes, literally. I walk outside the door frame and scan the area, but I don't see any children passing by. The only thing that greeted me at this open door was the morning sunshine's chilly breeze, which is making me feel a touch of death's life. I almost trod on a *manananggal* plastic toy that I see on the floor just in front of my feet. It seems like the kids were running away and left something here, and it dropped.

After bringing it inside my room, I lay on my bed in silence staring at it. Despite its half-crosswise chopped torso and bloodied eyes, I feel absolutely nothing when I gaze at it. Is all that has happened today fleeing my thoughts? The only thing I really need to do right now is study and go over everything we've covered in class for the past weeks. I want to do all of my schoolwork over this brief academic vacation. And so I thought.

I stock up on sweet treats as I study because they stimulate my brain and make me feel alive when reading and studying, particularly chocolates. At lunch, I cook some sweetened ham. I can't stop staring out the window, hoping the kids would return to get the toy. A few minutes later, my phone vibrates, and I receive a text from my father asking me to come back home.

"*Anak*, when will you come and visit us?" he asks.

I reply, "I have a lot of school work to do, *pa*. Maybe I cannot visit." But the 'maybe' will surely be 'not' at all.

I haven't received a reply from him since then. It is surely not a big deal.

I kept grinding hard at my homework until the clock read eleven o'clock. The *manananggal* toy slips from my grasp as I hurry to tidy up the table and put my school things back in their proper places. I step on it by mistake, and it absolutely crumbles to bits. Rolling my eyes, I sigh. I'll have to go out and get the same toy figure just in case the children want it back. I would like not to be the one to trigger their breakdown and to hear them calling on *mama*'s help.

Finally, it's the last week of November! A few days later, the Christmas songs of Mariah Carey and Jose Mari Chan started filling the ears of the customers as they rushed through the mall, buying presents to unwrap this coming twenty-fifth. I am in the department store right now and am currently lining up at the cashier. I had found exactly the same toy and decided to buy it. When it is finally my turn to pay, the cashier blinks twice, and her forehead creases as she stares at the toy.

Out of curiosity, she asks, "November has already passed, ma'am. What made you buy this for Christmas?"

I tell her a glimpse of the story behind it. She smiles and shares, "It reminds me of my children in the province. It's supposed to be a holiday, but I am not with them now."

I honestly don't know what to say, so I just smile at her back without showing my teeth.

It's finally Christmas Eve, and this toy is still with me. I haven't seen the children since that day they knocked on my door so I brought it with me here in my parent's house. I hang the toy on the Christmas tree instead.

There are a variety of foods and drinks that are arranged on the table, but what catches my attention was the *Jamon de Bola*. I remember having one in my apartment. It left there, frozen. My mom is busy entertaining the audience while helping with the food, while my father is helping move the *lechon* out of the fire.

I took a slice of the ham, and I couldn't stop admiring the thick, sweetened syrup that wrapped around it. My mom was about to reprimand me for eating ahead, but I cut her off with a question instead.

"How to make *Jamon de Bola, ma*?"

"I don't know, *anak*. But I know that the ham is made up of pig meat." My mom replies before she goes back and slips against her ankles. She falls on the ground and accidentally grabs the Christmas tree, which breaks some balls apart, including the *manananggal*. *Papa* refuses to help her stand up, making excuses that he is tired from roasting the pig, even though he sees mama struggling.

Oh, wait, I forgot—they're not together anymore.

The moment the family drills in, throwing up their deceitful words, I can't tear my eyes away from their beaming faces, which I know it's as unreal as the belief that *Jamon de Bola* gives luck. My father put on a show of giving care towards mom by dishing out a slice of ham onto her plate, all while my siblings have their eyes glued to his believable action.

I chuckle, giving a round of applause at the back of my head, dripping with sarcasm.

I happen to raise my chin, and it is a coincidence that I just noticed the *lechon* being laid on top of the table, surrounded by the food for the *Noche Buena*.

So, we just killed two lives to enjoy this night!

Café Latte

Coffee shops abound in the center of Cebu. Sean can also locate places offering only milk teas and various other beverages such as sodas and fruit juices. Individuals visit coffee shops to complete their assignments, organize important schedules, plan meetings, or brainstorm ideas. Initially, it served as a means of refreshment due to the city's climate, offering reprieve from the hot weather as a convenient way to consume a beverage in a cup. Enjoying coffee entails more than just holding the cup with a particular brand or consuming a drink that sustains us while we work on our laptops, particularly for college students like himself; it's a lifestyle.

"Cold café latte, please," Sean told the cashier—at the same time the barrister—about his order. Of course, he paired it with a blueberry cheesecake. He set up his tablet with its Bluetooth keyboard and USB-powered mouse. He started working on his pendings while waiting for his name to be called in the queue. Once called, he left his things on the table and went to get his drink. People inside the cafe won't bother stealing things that were not theirs—at least this is the fascinating thing he knows about this coffee culture. Perhaps they were also busy doing their own stuff, such as attending a Google or Zoom Meeting or doing some thesis. Sean could also spot law students reading their thick black books in a row with colorful sticker bookmarks hanging on the sides of the pages.

These were usually the scenarios in a coffee shop in Cebu. When he visited the province, one thing he looked forward to was finding a place to sip a coffee, especially since the internet connection was sometimes unstable. Every single instance where he connected his charger to an outlet in a coffee shop or when he dined at a single table in the bustling mini food court of a provincial mall to set up his digital canvas, there was an undeniable echo of dissatisfaction. Sean had harbored this naïve belief that by indulging in these actions—immersing himself in the unique flavors of coffee or milk tea distinct to each locale, even if they actually taste the same—he could somehow cloak his homesickness in comfort, lured into submission.

But, he was mistaken.

"Hot café latte, please," he ordered his favorite coffee, but right now, it was a hot version of it. Was it because he failed to comply with the cold one that made him dissatisfied? The taste was undeniably the same with a different brand in a different place… and a different temperature. He was relieved to finally take a break from city life. He thought that when he could take a sip of his favorite caffeine, he would finally feel at home. However, the kind of addiction that Sean was looking for was no longer to be found, and was perhaps cured by the essence of the fact that he was a foreigner in his own place.

Let's Eat *Lechon* in a Doll House

Christine was still in her condominium, even though it was already Christmas season. Malls started playing Jose Mari Chan's songs, and when she passed by the department store, she couldn't take her eyes off those parents who gifted their daughter a Barbie house. She ran into Santa Claus by mistake while he was dancing around the corner. Christine was so drawn to that Barbie house that she didn't notice the dancing people in the middle.

"Ho! Ho! Ho! Merry Christmas!" Santa Claus greeted her while rubbing his stomach and leaning against the air. She stepped back and looked away as soon as she felt the eyes of the crowd watching her. Their eyes were like balls hanging from the Christmas tree—wide, sparkling, but lifeless. She apologized to Santa Claus without looking at him, but right before she could step out from the middle, he followed.

He asked Christine what her wish for Christmas was, and she was stunned. Her lips tightened, and was speechless. The last time she heard this question was when she was ten years old. Christine is now in her twenties, and she didn't expect this question to still exist. Her jaw hung wide open as her eyes stuck at his, thinking about the answer to which she should reply.

"To have good grades in my finals," Christine replied. Honestly, she just recently finished her first semester, and for the past few weeks, she had been working on her finals. She even turned-in her one requirement yesterday to finish her last project before Christmas Eve.

This holiday season doesn't feel any different.

Santa sent her luck, saying that her wish was granted. After this encounter, Christine went to a grocery store to restock her needs. She noticed *ispageti*, *Keso de Bola*, and *Jamon de Bola* on families' shopping carts. She glanced in her basket at the oatmeal, fresh milk, *kalamay*, and fruit juices she picked. Since none of these items were tied to Christmas, Christine bought a kilo of roasted pork for a meal at an outlet store. Long lines made buying one take an hour. At least she found something she could bring and eat for the occasion.

It was already evening. She sat in front of her table with the food she prepared to eat *alone*, especially the *Lechon*. Her phone vibrated, and the results of her grades were shown. Santa Claus seemed to have really granted her wish.

"Merry Christmas, *mama* and *papa*!" It was like these voices from the other units were shaking the walls. Christine tasted the *Lechon*, and it was a bit bitter.

She stared at herself in the mirror. She had been diligent about her health, food intake, and skincare. She also passed all subjects this first semester, and so she laughed. In terms of her fulfilment, Christine has never seen herself radiate with such brilliance before. She sighs in relief for who she is right now, even though she wishes she could have experienced eating this *Lechon* inside Barbie's house.

Behind the Steps of Cooking
Ginisang Kalabasa

I overslept for intramurals and missed out on what was happening at school the whole morning. My dad quickly gave me a ride, and when I got there, I noticed a lady guard standing in the path of the only available parking spot left. My dad had to step out to ask her what was going on, but as soon as we both turned our attention back to the lady, she disappeared. My father and I talked about what was happening, but we agreed to just let it go.

"Since Halloween is around the corner, it's natural to encounter such things," he reasoned out with a chuckle.

During lunch, I noticed our school guards huddled together in the corner, engaging in casual conversation and enjoying their meal. However, none of them looked like the female guard we encountered in the parking lot. I mean, they were all males, so I asked one of them about a female guard, and he became silent. He said that the last time they had a female guard was seven years ago. She passed away because of a car accident. She rescued a grade school student from crossing the road, which led her to death. The friends I know who have been here for almost ten years said they had only heard a little about her. I was absolutely floored; I couldn't utter a word.

I shared it with my dad, and he convinced me to talk me out of believing in those things. But deep down, I wondered how quickly people are forgotten after a person splits their soul from their body. I headed home, mulling over what had just occurred. We swung by the market to grab some grub for dinner, and I noticed a heap of *kalabasa* in the distance that resembled pumpkins. I had a lightbulb moment and knew exactly what to cook. Moreover, pumpkins are ideal for Halloween decorations as well. I was hitting two birds with one stone.

My mom cooked *Ginisang Kalabasa*. As she slices the *kalabasa*, it feels like fragments of memories were being torn apart that day. Every seed that was removed was the shattered bones of the lady guard, resting inside the coffin. The aroma of sautéed garlic and onion is reminiscent of forgotten souls. Adding shredded dried fish and quickly cooking it before adding the *kalabasa* gives it a touch of an anesthetic view of death. Once the beans have been stirred for two minutes, it hits me how quickly her death has passed. When the water had evaporated completely, the haunting memory of this day vanished.

Finally, the dish has been served, and my mom added a dash of ground black pepper to enhance the flavor of the meal. I decided to pair it with some steaming, hot rice. The aroma of the dish screams nutrients and takes me back to the authentic spirit of the Halloween season. It satisfies our hunger and gives birth to a hero who rescued a child.

Part Two - The Bottom: Served Below

Glory Cabilete

The Lockdown Offering

Waking up is like stepping into a world of endless possibilities, where every dawn brings a fresh start. However, it also unlocks Pandora's box of challenges, where one must brace oneself for the potential pitfalls and the opportunities of facing setbacks, humiliation, or heartbreak. To wake up without knowing the context behind having to sleep, not even the exact time, is a phenomenon that grasps excitement; it adds flavor to my purpose. These things were, without a shadow of a doubt, as alien as those lurking outside the space—fate to exist.

There may have been a lack of clarity and an abundance of questions—a huge wonder about existence. Perhaps I can overhear them using languages and practicing customs that are unusual to me and might pose a threat to my entrenched ideologies or sustenance that are poison to the human system. But it doesn't mean that these would hinder me from being humble and human enough to appreciate and acknowledge the reality that our world does not exist with Earth alone, but with the entire universe.

Hence, I could see myself trying to communicate with them through the spirit of love and humility. I've got a burning desire to gain knowledge, to bridge the gap between us, and to delve into their culture and the roots of their existence. I could picture myself asking for food not because I want to ease my hunger; it was for me to ask them to feed me with the differences they have that we, as human beings, are ignorant about. But it will surely not be the subject of dealing with these aliens that made my day difficult; it will certainly be about accepting that reality is broad and life is a mystery and we hold the responsibility to consume it or die.

Yes, life and human interaction are riddles to be solved, including the presence of these aliens. I, too, for sure feels like an alien, trapped in this ubiquitous foreign world where interpersonal communication declines and digital media serves as the sole means of human bonding. I found myself reflecting in the glass mirror and couldn't identify who I was, and when I stepped my foot outside my house or rather, the alien's spaceship, all I could see were unfamiliar, strange faces lurking at every corner. There was no chemistry between us, at least that I could tell. It's as if I were cut off from the world I once knew, and now I can't decide if I'm the alien here or if everyone else is—or maybe it was *life* itself, dressed for human satisfaction, that was the alien?

At the end, my relationship with these aliens slowly falls down like a mask, uncovering their unfamiliar faces into recognizable ones. Then, with these interactions, I could share it with the world I live in, and it would undoubtedly form a story worth telling and a history worth remembering.

Pizza Delivery

The day after my twin sister died, the family sank into total slumber. My parents weren't communicating as usual and I was left alone in this home as if I had never existed. I dine and live with my own silence as I start missing my sister every minute. I spotted, through the hole in my door, that my parents arrived while chatting to a man wearing a white clothing and a metallic object wrapped around his neck. I sensed my heart palpitating louder than I ever imagined; tears slowly began to pour down as I could feel the side of my forehead soaking.

My dad wouldn't stop yelling at the guy in the white suit, and my mom wouldn't stop weeping! I hid from the corner of the wall, but the worried doctor saw me peeking around the corner at them while they argued.

I fled.

They yelled out in a fit of rage. Intensely repeating my name in a loud voice was grating on my ears. I could feel their words digging further into my eardrums, as if they were doing it on purpose to render me deaf. I covered my ears and tried to get away from their bickering until I had reached the garden. I quickly closed the doors to lock my parents from the outside. Coincidentally, I heard a chime from the front door, alerting us that a person was waiting outside. My parents exchanged troubled glances, anxiety etched across their foreheads, while that man stood behind them, urging them to calm down.

As I advanced toward the direct route to the main door, the reverberating thud of the door's translucent construction filled my ears. The more I moved, the closer I felt to sovereignty. When I spotted a hammer beside the plant as I stepped back from the entrance, an evil smile plastered on my face.

My mother became alarmed and hollered at me to put down the hammer from my hand as soon as I had grabbed it. However, my father was adamant to use his methods for unlocking the doors without breaking the glass. My parents needed assistance, but the white-clad guy who often stopped by the home did nothing except glaring at me.

It seemed like the bell would never stop. While reaching for the doorknob, I felt a trembling sensation spread across my whole fingers.

Every second counts until I can fling open the door...

I let out a gasp. My parents had stopped me in an attempt to prevent me from doing my plans, but they arrived too late. As I opened the main entrance, the chilly wind engulfed my body. The only thing blocking my path was a few pizza boxes stacking up. With curiosity, I blinked my eyes numerous times. So, I have refrained from engaging in any aggressive acts, as my parents expected me to be.

"Who ordered these?" My mother questioned us while simultaneously lifting both of her eyebrows and her shoulders as she gazed at my father and I.

My dad was quick to respond by shaking his head and exclaiming, "Not me!" After that, he went on to check outside since none of us had seen *that* someone who had delivered this to us.

As soon as I realized that there was no one else around, I cut off my father in his first few syllables. "Honey, I think we should call a police—"

"Hm!" I chuckled long before they could point their eyes at me as someone who may have left the house to order these enormous boxes. "It's Maria…"

My mother and father exchanged bewildered glances with one another as they tried to make sense of what had just happened. They asked in unison, "Who is

Maria?" My irises expanded, and I swiftly shifted my gaze in their direction.

With my head tilted to the other side, I explained, "She is my identical twin. You have forgotten her?" My parents gasped in wonder. The atmosphere began to feel oppressive as the wind had a drying effect on our hair, and the sky became more overcast. I can feel the chills choking my throat. Everyone raised their eyes to the heavens and checked the weather with their fingertips.

I yawned, and as soon as my parents' eyes met mine, I asked my father, "Dad, please carry these boxes towards my sister's room. I'll arrange them later; I have to get some sleep—"

"Sweetie, you don't have a sister…"

I stared at them with a creased forehead. "Huh? What are you talking about? She's in the room." It was like there was a squeeze inside of my heart that felt like a safety pin digging, but it was causing wounds. I wanted to avoid the inconvenience of having to hear what they had to say, so I left. They called out my name one more time, expecting me to turn around and talk to them, but I did not allow it to influence me in any way.

Their voices cracked in pain.

—

Sitting here in front of these cardboards gave me an upset stomach. I had always been cautious about not engaging in discussion with my parents, so I would pretend to sleep and sneak into my sister's bed whenever they were not around. When I began unpacking the boxes, my soul was on the verge of escaping my body when the window suddenly opened with a bang. I was taken aback when I realized that I had accidently struck one of the boxes, crashing it to the ground.

The lid of the package I was opening unexpectedly came off, and the pizza dough spilled onto the floor. However, I heard the clinking sound of a pizza cutter rolled *just* out of nowhere. My eardrums are being shaken by its metallic sound that I had to jerk my head to stop myself from becoming annoyed. It rolled over toward the door as it slowly opened all of a sudden, perhaps as a result of the power that the wind was exerting.

I followed where my eyes led until I saw the gleeful face of my twin sister. I was barely capable of seeing out the general contours of her face as the wind swept its way around my neck. She seemed to have just gotten home from college since she was clothed in her uniform and her skirt almost filled with ketchup. She took a few moments to pick up the cutter before tossing it out to the side in a playful gesture.

"Does the pizza taste good?" She asked, her smile extending all the way to her earlobes. My heart exploded with happiness. I took the first few steps toward her in a running motion, but she interrupted me by holding up her fingers in a stop sign gesture.

My eyebrows furrowed in disbelief, but she only smirked and shook her head as she stepped closer to me instead of responding to my expression. She beamed with the loveliest of all smiles, one that I had been yearning for but had nearly forgotten existed. That reassuring look that brought me happy memories of my youth.

"I always know you're not dead." She gave a sour grimace before speaking.

"Well, I feel like one every day."

I was about to ask her some more questions when she suddenly turned her attention to the boxes and requested my help in reorganizing her belongings. And because her room was in such a disorganized state, as if it were not owned by a female like her, we spent nearly half of the day tidying it up.

The rest of the time, my sister asked me to visit those places we visited when we were still children. We rode a rollercoaster, sang in a karaoke, dropped in the amusement park, watched those animals in the zoo, and a lot more exciting things. We shared the same laughter, joys, and pains especially when we discussed our previous lives.

When we arrived home, both of us were still laughing. I headed to the entrance first before I opened it, I looked back to her and said, "I can't wait to see our parents' reaction when they see you. They would be happy for sure."

She smiled... *A little*.

As I began inserting the key to the door and had unlocked it, I turned back to her with excitement. However, just as I was starting to grasp how much pleasure it was to bring her home again, she vanished into thin air.

—

My alarm clock woke me up this morning. I quickly looked around for my sister, but she wasn't here. I stretched my arms and suddenly noticed that I was holding a pizza cutter.

What is this thing doing here?

I went downstairs and told my parents about my sister. But, they showed me a blank expression saying that I don't have one. "You really want to have a sister? Anyway, here, eat some!"

I felt confused. I looked at my reflection from the cutter before I slowly looked at it closer and was flustered when I saw the reflection of myself from the present; sad, depressed, and lonely.

"M-Maria?"

Happy Birthday

BREAKING NEWS: Several individuals had gone missing; some of them were found dead with body parts being separated.

This news had resurfaced again across the whole city, and I had a suspicion that one of the murders was a friend of mine. I dine in my silence as I start doubting about my friend's weird actions, like calling different people at night with her soft, low, and suspicious voice as if she was hiding something. Whenever she catches me listening, she quickly drops the call.

She always arrives at midnight with blood stains on her apron while carrying a bunch of meat with its blood still dripping on the ground. I sensed my heart palpitating louder than I ever imagined; tears slowly began to pour down as I could feel the side of my forehead soaking.

Another night had arrived, and I witnessed her yelling out in a fit of rage. Intensely uttering words that I couldn't understand since she did this behind closed doors—I wouldn't be able to hear them properly. I could feel her words digging further into my eardrums, as if they were doing it on purpose to render me deaf. I covered my ears and tried to get away from her bickering until I peeked into the kitchen and saw her chopping some bones again! I let out troubled glances, anxiety etched across my forehead, while rushing myself back to my room to get my phone and take some pictures for evidence.

As I advanced toward the direct route to the main door, the reverberating thud of the door's translucent construction filled my ears. It turned out that she heard me running from a distance, and so I was filled with horror when I saw her reflection standing at my near side!

Our eyes met.

She pressed the knife against her back and covered her wounded fingers behind her. Even though it was dark, I couldn't help but notice that her eyes were extremely wide open. She had blood on her feet, and when she saw that I had noticed it, she hurriedly covered her toes next to the other one. I quickly batted my eyelids a few times as my hands frantically searched for any excuses.

I responded to her by saying, "I-I am trying to complete my school work, which is why I am taking videos!" I immediately shifted the camera so that it was recording from my vantage point, and I let her see it. "Look! I am taking videos of myself!"

It wasn't clear to me whether or not she would believe me, but please, I hope she would not murder me! She looked at me with eyes filled with suspicion as she continued to gaze at me. She even protruded her chin and stood tall in an assertive way. My nose was contaminated with the scent of blood, and I had to hold on to myself to keep from throwing up.

She advised with an air of composure, "Make it quick, and after that, make sure that you will sleep as early as possible." But, despite the seeming peace, I couldn't help but feel apprehensive. To begin, I don't see why she would suggest that I go to sleep early. When she was aware that I was now working on a school assignment, she never once told me like this!

What if she plans to murder me later on? That is why she is asking me to sleep! She wants my flesh to have a fresh appearance and be in good condition so that she can sell it for a greater price... *Perhaps?!*

"Y-Yes..." I responded to her in such acute anxiety that I could even hear my heart thumping out loud as it raced through my chest. As soon as she walked out of the room, I let out a huge sigh of relief. Before I stood up and saved the recordings to my Google Drive, I made sure the door was locked first.

She came home with a wound on her face a day before my birthday, at the same hour at night. She seemed fatigued, particularly since she had dark bags under her eyes, and while she was walking toward her room, she even went off balance. I asked her with boldness as to where she came from, but she did not answer my question. She just paused for a few seconds without glancing in my direction, which caused me to gulp. But, after that, she entered her room without saying a single word.

Since our rooms were close together, the only thing that separated us was the wall in the middle. She was chopping things that sounded too violent for me to hear. I even heard her yelling that the meat looked delicious and that she can't wait to eat it, which made my whole soul leap up and down with nervousness.

I took an audio recording of her voice and saved it to my phone again.

Early this morning, November 1st, the doorbell rang. As I reached for the doorknob, I became cognizant of a quivering feeling that was spreading throughout all of my fingers. Because she had not engaged in conversation with me for several days at this point, I couldn't help but be flabbergasted and felt the need to call the police someday. Today is my birthday, but it seemed as if I wouldn't be able to enjoy it, at least for the time being, due to this struggle.

'Who ordered these?" Immediately after opening the door and seeing a box, I questioned the delivery person about it.

"Miss Anika Becker," he replied. Yes, Anika is the name of my friend.

I took a deep sigh and then made myself take the package against my instincts. Even though she had indicated on the delivery form that if she was unavailable to sign the papers, it was her intention for me to do it in her stead.

I hastily opened the package, even though it said *do not open it*, as soon as I arrived on the terrace, just in case Anika intended to send me a bomb here; thus, I am at least somewhat *safe*. It was also strange for her to get out this morning since, for the prior several days, again, I had always caught her getting out like a serial murderer at night.

I was curious as to what she was doing at this point.

When I opened the box, I found several sharp things inside, such as little knives, pizza cutters, can openers, barbecue spears, and a lot of other similar items. In addition to that, there were these eerie masks of various monstrosities and candles. Even though there were these paper plates, which I couldn't make sense of in terms of their significance, the fact that these spooky things were here was sufficient for me to be frightened about my safety while I was with her.

I took a few steps back and quickly closed the box when I noticed a large knife that could cut through a substantial and extensive amount of the bones of an animal. I put it near her room, which she had closed for the last week, and I have not visited that area of the house since she is refusing to let me in even if I insisted. After that, I ran to the kitchen to get some cold water from the refrigerator.

When I looked in the refrigerator and saw that it was full of cooked flesh and waste bones, I let out an unintended scream as I realized what I was seeing for the first time. The hairs that normally resided in my skin began to stand on end.

I quickly left the apartment and made my way to the local police station to file a complaint about her behavior. It took me nearly two hours before the policemen would believe what I was reporting, even if I had sent them my documentation as well as the video recordings.

The cops were right behind me as I climbed the stairs to our apartment. When I saw that the door wasn't locked, I was taken aback, and when I opened it, I was utterly at a loss for words when I saw who welcomed me from the inside.

"HAPPY BIRTHDAY!" Anika welcomed me with a huge smile on her face as her companions were gathered around the large table that was laden with meal preparations. Party poppers rained down on my face, as well as on the police officers who were with me.

My jaw dropped in wonder. I asked, "W-What is this?"

Even though the police officers' presence confused her, Anika responded, "I was working on this surprise for you days before your birthday. Our friends helped me too." I explained to her my suspicion, and she just laughed at me. She clarified that she was just preventing me from getting spoiled by the surprise.

What have I done?

Devoured by Death

The dazzling stars of the suspended chandelier stole my sight as I gazed upon its majestic presence, breathing vitality and encouragement into the attendees at the grand gathering in the hotel's event hall. It wasn't just the chandelier's lights that caught my attention, but also the sight of that lone gentleman in a tuxedo, sipping champagne from a distance. His eyes resembled sparkling chandeliers, and his charisma was so vast that it stood out amidst the crowd. I pictured myself twirling under the moon's glow with him as I approached the ripe age of eighteen. The ticking hands of the clock were surely impatient, unwilling to delay the onset of this golden chance. I took the plunge and went up to him, and his smile pulled me in like an iron string that keeps the chandelier from floating.

"Hi, handsome man," I swiftly retorted with a counter-smile matching his energy. I couldn't wrap my head around his behavior toward a mere acquaintance. I wondered if he's also like this with people.

He lifted his bubbly-filled glass and pointed out an empty chair beside him. "Have a seat. Let's wet our whistles, young lady," he said, pulling up a chair from under the bar. Wow, that invitation to drink with him came in the blink of an eye from this dashing gentleman.

I followed him. The music struck up, but it couldn't hold a flicker of note to the thunderous rhythm of my heart beside him. And being the lone damsel seated beside him, he extended his hand, beckoning me to partake in a merry dance, to which I gleefully obliged. "Take my hand; it's time to dance," he whispered in my face. His eyes couldn't let go of mine.

As we hit the dance floor beneath the chandelier, it dawned on me that the moonlight was the truth that sparked our connection. It's nearly the stroke of midnight, and I'm counting down the hours until I come of age. When he had me in his grasp, he leaned in and took a whiff. He then whispered, "You were as fragrant as a gentle breeze beneath the moon's glow."

I chuckled. "Maybe because I'm on the cusp of reaching eighteen."

His eyes were glued. "You have no idea how thrilled I am to hit that milestone," I chimed in. He reeled me in, nearly knocking me off balance. "I can read the sparkle in your eyes; it's written all over your face," he grinned. "I'm about to become the alpha in a tribe real soon. I, too, am as excited as you," he said, blending his words before he gave me a wink.

My jaw dropped a mile after hearing this. But what really grabbed my eye was the way his serious yet precious peepers locked onto mine after dropping that last statement. He wasn't an alpha yet, but he grinned at me as if he were. He swallowed the canary, hinting at a secret too obvious to be concealed even by the darkest night.

Does he want me to be his Luna?

He twirled me in the moon's glow until I landed on a cloud-like mattress. The room was as dark as the moon's shadow on its way to becoming full. All I could hear was our laughter, the sweet melody that danced through the air, the only tune that graced my ears amidst this lively music at this party.

I laid down with him on top of mine. He rubbed noses with me and showered me with gentle kisses, then made his way down to my neck. He explored each and every corner of my body, paying special attention to my fingertips. He lifted his head high and set his sights back on my lips. Right now, he is inserting his tongue.

I couldn't help but let out soft whispers of delight due to his actions toward me.

"You're so fresh. Really, really fresh," he whispered in between kisses.

When our gazes intertwined, he wore a sly grin and set a passionate kiss on me, causing my body to jolt and keep pace with his speed. "I hope you'll be my significant other when the stars align," he murmured in my ear.

"Whoever fate pairs me with, I'll wholeheartedly give myself to him. If you're the one, it'll be the greatest gift of my eighteenth birthday," I responded, never breaking eye contact.

With our hearts beating in sync, the only sound that reached my ears from beyond the walls was the symphony of our passionate love. It was a breath of fresh air, a hidden gem that will forever hold a special place in my heart. It wasn't the chandelier but rather the moonlight that stood witness to the promises we made.

—

The shrill call from my phone, which broke through the total darkness, startled me out of sleep. I blinked multiple times, and when I cast my gaze upon the man I crossed paths with last evening, he wasn't there. I had a moment of heart in my mouth, thinking it was all just a figment of my imagination. I cast my gaze upon my phone and beheld my father calling. Bugs were dancing in my stomach as the ringtone remained silent while a whirlwind of commotion unfolded just beyond my reach. So, I answered the phone call instead.

"Hello, dad, what's the matter?"

"Elaine! Our tribe has been attacked! They are aiming for you now. Please, run away!"

My senses were hijacked by my father's voice in a state of panic, especially when I caught wind of a tumultuous uproar from the rear and the piercing cries of lives being snatched away. My hands were trembling, and my heart was on the verge of breaking.

"Where are you right now?"

And before my dad could answer, all I could hear was his voice screaming at the top of his lungs, piercing through the air like a knife, accompanied by the eerie scratching sounds of the werewolves. Without me even realizing it, my phone slipped through my fingers. I quickly changed and slipped away from the hotel before anyone from that attacking tribe could find me.

As I made a hasty retreat from the hotel, leaping from window to window, little did I know that my father's ringtone would be his screaming voice of death.

I found myself in a race through the woods, with the thunderous footsteps of werewolves from my back. There were countless of them, and I wouldn't be surprised if they could bring me to my knees in a heartbeat. I gazed upon the sun, casting its rays through the leafy portals, and it brought to mind the radiant chandelier and amorous moonlight I encountered last evening.

Life is totally unexpected.

"Elaine! Elaine!" I heard some of them shouting my name. The rhythm of their voices didn't quite hit my hopefulness like the music that tickled my ears last night. It didn't hold a candle to the sweet kisses bestowed upon me by that man, whose name I didn't even have a chance to know!

Out of the blue, my eyes caught sight of a colossal beam emanating from the horizon, only to realize I had reached the mountain's cliff. I had hope in my eyes when I saw the light, but it turned out to be a false dawn. I stopped running and sauntered towards the edge, peering into the depths below. I took a step back and watched in awe as the rock plummeted into the abyss. I couldn't believe my eyes.

My heart was racing to a different tune than the one I heard last night. This wasn't the rhythm I was hoping to dance to. I glanced over my shoulder and had a gut feeling that this tribe and their werewolves would surely catch me alive. There was nowhere else to turn. In the blink of an eye, I remembered that man's promise. I cast my gaze beyond the sun as it radiated with even greater brilliance. I was torn between holding onto the same promises, but if the moonlight bore witness to our vows, then this sunlight would surely speak my desires to the moon.

Long before the enemy could catch me, I took a *leap of faith* off the cliff.

—

A few days after the wake of the attack, the pack came together to pay their respects and grieve the loss of their leader and his daughter, and the far-flung relatives and comrades assembled to shower their final thoughts and blossoms, and the mysterious man Elaine encountered at the hotel sauntered in, wearing a huge hat that concealed his visage. Like the devastating spirit of the attack, he was clad in ebony attire. He stood before Elaine's grave, placing a bouquet of flowers on the hallowed ground. This bouquet was the only ray of warmth in the midst of a stiff wilderness.

He locked eyes with the inscription and spoke its words in hushed tones.

"Here's a wine for your freedom!"
He then added, "Cheers!"

The Kitchen: A Brief Outro

The wafting simmer of pots and the sizzle of frying pans flare up, sending haunting wisps of scent to your nostrils' doors, knocking your senses beneath the lamp of moonlight.

These steam in white cloaks draw you toward the kitchen, stirring daydreams summoned by life's endless, lurking appetite for sustenance—*where hunger waits* beneath the sleepless apparition of your growling stomach.

Words After Eating

After you have read the stories and devoured the meals offered, I hope you all have a nutritious experience. Before we stand and leave the table, I wish to give my gratitude to the following:

- To Arcturus Gonzales, the outside chef of the stories, I thank you for your insights in sprinkling a seasoning of validation towards the recipes provided in each bite.

- To Gian Capitan, the kitchen's living freezer of a cook's dilemmas and impulsive overthinking of the right ingredients to use in every fry, simmer, or grill, I am very grateful to have your presence and encouragement.

- To Jozef Guantero, the visualizer who garnished every plate before being served, I appreciate your time and effort in making the book cover of *Where Hunger Waits* appealing to the diners' appetite.

- To the organizers and speakers of the *Food for Life: Lessons from the Garden* conference held last November 2023, this event inspired me to prepare a book to be presented to the readers. Thus, it allows *Where Hunger Waits* to be tasted by its right readership.

- To Ukiyoto Publishing, thank you for being the kitchen of this creative cookbook of life and stories, which opens the door to different taste buds.

- To the food lovers, may you find your own kind of memories in every food you intake and grapple with all the chewing and swallowing you can do to make every minute of your loved ones worth it and not wasted.

- To the lovers of fiction, may your love for literature flourish and extend beyond the boundaries of what you can only consume and nourish. Your support is highly appreciated, even in the eyes behind the kitchen table.

May these stories be added to nutrition in your lives and continue to support the dynamism made through written art.

See you in the next story.

About the Author

Glory Cabilete

Glory Cabilete is currently pursuing a BA in Literary and Cultural Studies at the University of San Carlos. She's the author of a poetry collection entitled "Mathematics is a Woman" with its translation in Filipino to be published under Ukiyoto Publishing, and novels under the pseudonym of Purple Glory such as "His Destined Mate," and "Dwell with Snaedis" (Beautiful Disaster). Also, she collaborated on Magkasintahan 2.0 Volume XI and Magkasintahan 3.0 Volume IX with Ukiyoto Publishing, where she wrote "Revolutionary Ardor," "Perfect Bathrobe," and "Made of Monochrome," which are poems that navigate women's experiences and gender struggles. Her upcoming publication of a flash fiction collection, "Mathematics is a Woman: Fluid Dynamics," is a book to look forward to this 2025.